STECK-VAUGHN

PAIR-IT BOOKS™

The Apple Pie Family

Written by Gare Thompson
Illustrated by Winifred Barnum-Newman

STECK-VAUGHN
COMPANY

A Division of Harcourt Brace & Company

Our family loves to make apple pies.

Grandma and Grandpa grow apples.

3

We help pick the apples.

We fill up many baskets.

We wash the apples.

We peel the apples.

We sift the flour.

We pour the milk.

We roll out the dough.

We put it in the pans.

We add the apples.

We measure the sugar.

We put the pies in the oven.

We cook them slowly.

We eat them quickly!